This edition published by Parragon in 2012
Parragon
Queen Street House
4 Queen Street
Bath BA1 1HE, UK
www.parragon.com

ISBN 978-1-4454-7736-7

Printed in China

THE JUNGLE BOOK

Bath • New York • Singapore • Hong Kong • Cologne • Delhi
Melbourne • Amsterdam • Johannesburg • Auckland • Shenzhen

Deep in the jungle, Bagheera the panther was out hunting. Suddenly, he heard a strange crying sound coming from the river.

He followed the sound and discovered a basket with a tiny baby boy inside.

"Why, it's a Man-cub!" he said. "This little chap needs food and a mother's care. Perhaps Mother Wolf will look after him."

Mother Wolf agreed to help. They named the Man-cub
Mowgli and he grew up safe and happy in the jungle.

But everything changed when Mowgli was ten years old. Shere Khan, the man-eating tiger, heard about the Man-cub and came searching for him.

The wolves agreed that Bagheera should take the boy back to the Man-village where he would be safe.

So the next morning, Bagheera and Mowgli set off on their long journey. Mowgli was angry and upset. He didn't want to leave his home in the jungle.

When darkness fell, Bagheera and Mowgli climbed a
tree and settled down to sleep on a branch. Nearby,
hiding under some leaves, was Kaa, the python.

    As soon as Bagheera was asleep, Kaa slithered
towards the Man-cub. His shining eyes seemed to have
a magic power and Mowgli quickly began to sink into a
deep trance.

Slowly, Kaa started to wind himself around the boy,
ready to swallow him up!

Suddenly, Bagheera woke up and sprang at
Kaa. He struck the snake with his claws and sent him
slithering away into the jungle.

At dawn, Mowgli was woken by a very loud noise. He looked down from the tree and saw Colonel Hathi and the Dawn Patrol marching along.

"Up, two, three, four! Up, two, three, four!" trumpeted the elephant.

Mowgli jumped down from the tree, got on all fours and joined the end of the parade behind a baby elephant. He had great fun, copying everything the little elephant did!

Eventually, Bagheera caught up with Mowgli and
wanted to carry on towards the Man-village.

    But Mowgli refused to go. He grabbed hold of a
tree trunk and held on tightly.

    Bagheera was very cross and ran off, leaving the
Man-cub all alone.

It wasn't long before Mowgli met a friendly bear called Baloo. He told Baloo how much he wanted to stay in the jungle.

"No problem!" Baloo said, "I'll look after you!"

Baloo enjoyed teaching his new friend all about the 'bare necessities of life.' Soon, Mowgli could fight like a bear, growl like a bear and even scratch like a bear!

Later that afternoon, Mowgli and Baloo waded into the river to keep cool. Mowgli sat on Baloo's tummy as they gently floated along. It was very peaceful and Baloo soon fell asleep.

But watching from some trees was a group of monkeys who were waiting to kidnap Mowgli.

The monkeys sprang out from their hiding place and grabbed the Man-cub.

Baloo woke with a jump but it was too late! The monkeys were already carrying Mowgli off to the ruined temple where they lived.

Luckily, Bagheera heard Mowgli's cries and rushed to the river to help. He found Baloo, who explained what had happened.

"We need a rescue plan," Bagheera said.

At the ruined temple, Louie, King of the Apes, was
sitting on his throne waiting for the Man-cub to arrive.

"So, you're here at last!" Louie cried, as Mowgli was
dropped beside him.

Louie offered to help Mowgli stay in the jungle.
In return, he wanted to learn the secret of Man's red fire.

But before Mowgli could explain that he didn't know
the secret, Louie declared that they would have a great feast
in honor of their guest.

Baloo and Bagheera reached the temple just in time to see Louie leap from his throne and start to sing and dance in celebration of the Man-cub's arrival.

As Mowgli's feet began to tap to the music, he forgot his troubles and joined in the fun.

"Baloo," whispered Bagheera. "You distract the monkeys while I rescue Mowgli."

Baloo had an idea…He dressed in some coconut shells and leaves to make himself look like a lady ape. Then he waved at Louie.

The King thought the lady ape was very beautiful and rushed over to ask her to dance. He had no idea that it was really Baloo in disguise!

But as Baloo danced, his disguise began to fall off. The angry monkeys realized they had been tricked and started to attack him.

Just as Bagheera rushed over to help, Baloo knocked over a pillar.

The temple came crashing down on top of the monkeys. Luckily, Baloo and Bagheera managed to drag Mowgli to safety. The three friends ran deep into the jungle and found a place to rest.

That night, Bagheera and Baloo kept watch over Mowgli as he slept.

It was time to discuss their young friend's future . . .

"The Man-cub must go to the Man-village," said
Bagheera, "It's not safe for him to stay in the jungle."

Baloo, remembering Shere Khan, had to admit that
Bagheera was right.

So the next morning, Baloo led Mowgli off towards
the Man-village.

When the Man-cub found out where they were headed, he was very angry.

"You don't want me to stay—you're just like Bagheera!" he shouted.

But before Baloo could explain, Mowgli ran off into the jungle.

It wasn't long before Shere Khan spotted Mowgli in the distance. Emerging from the shadows, the tiger gave a loud roar.

He leaped at Mowgli, taking the Man-cub by surprise.

But Shere Khan stopped in mid-leap and fell to the
ground—Baloo had caught him by the tail!

Shere Khan roared with rage as he dragged Baloo
behind him, but the brave bear was determined not to
let go.

Eventually, the furious tiger managed to flip
Baloo over his head. The bear hit the ground with a
mighty crash.

Mowgli ran over to Baloo, who was lying very still on the ground.

"Please get up, Baloo!" he cried.

Bagheera came over to comfort Mowgli. "Baloo was very brave," the panther said.

"Was?" gulped Mowgli. "You mean...Baloo's dead?"

But before Bagheera had a chance to reply, Baloo sat up and rubbed his eyes. He wasn't dead after all!

Mowgli laughed and threw his arms round the big bear's neck.

Suddenly, a lightning bolt struck a nearby tree, which
burst into flames. Shere Khan was terrified! Fire was the
only thing that frightened him.

Seeing his chance to get back at the tiger, Mowgli
picked up a burning branch. The Man-cub tied the
burning branch to the tiger's tail.

Shere Khan screamed as he clawed the branch
away. Then he fled into the jungle—never to be
seen again!

The three friends carried on towards the Man-village. Suddenly, they heard someone singing across the river.

Mowgli peered through the trees and saw a young girl kneeling by the river.

"Isn't she pretty!" cried Mowgli, climbing a tree to have a closer look. The girl turned and smiled. Mowgli shyly smiled back. When she began to walk off towards the Man-village, Mowgli ran to join her.

Baloo and Bagheera felt very sad that their young friend was leaving. But they knew he would now be happy and safe.

"It's where he belongs," sighed Bagheera. "Come on Baloo, let's get back to where we belong."

And so the two friends headed back towards the jungle, singing and dancing happily.